# Horrible Baby

by Jean Ure

Illustrated by
Joanna Graham

## CHAPTER 1

"Sophie," said Sophie's mum, quite crossly. "I've already told you three times ... don't keep banging about like that! You'll wake the baby."

Horrible baby. *Stupid* baby. Sophie picked up her doll and threw it savagely across the room. 'Crash!' went the doll, knocking a plate off the table.

"*Sophie!*" Sophie's mum turned round, angrily. The baby opened its mouth and began to cry. "Now look what you've done! *And* I'd only just got her to sleep!"

If it wanted to sleep it ought to be in a bedroom, not cluttering up the rest of the house. Sophie picked up her doll and cuddled it, tenderly.

Mum flew at the baby and began to make cooing noises. Everyone was always making cooing noises at it. Whenever they went shopping silly old ladies kept stopping to peer in at the pram and gurgle and cluck.

Oh, what a lovely baby! What a pretty little thing!

Once upon a time, before the horrible baby had come, they had said that Sophie was a pretty little thing. Now nobody took any notice of Sophie, it was all for the baby. And the baby wasn't pretty, it was bald and red-faced and ugly. *And* it smelt of sick. *And* it was always messing up its nappies. Ugh!

"I'm very ashamed of you," said Mum. "You're old enough to know better." She wasn't talking about the baby messing its nappies, she was talking about Sophie misbehaving.

"I thought you'd be happy to have a new little sister ... I thought you'd want to help me with her."

Help? With that horrible smelly thing? Sophie would rather give first aid to a slug.

The telephone started to ring.

"Tell her you're sorry," said Sophie's mum. "And talk to her nicely."

Mum went out into the hall to answer the telephone.

Sophie stamped over to look at the baby.

"I hate you," said Sophie. The baby smiled and waved its fingers. "Stupid," said Sophie.

Mum came back into the room. "That was your daddy," she said. "He sent you his love, but I told him you didn't deserve it ... you're being a very unpleasant little girl."

Sophie sulked. It wasn't her fault. She hadn't asked for a new baby.

By the end of the day Sophie had

gone shopping with Mum and been forced to watch while all the shop assistants cooed over the baby,

disgraced herself by throwing a tantrum in the supermarket because she wasn't allowed to have a bar of chocolate,

gone to visit Gran and been forced to watch while Gran cooed over the baby.

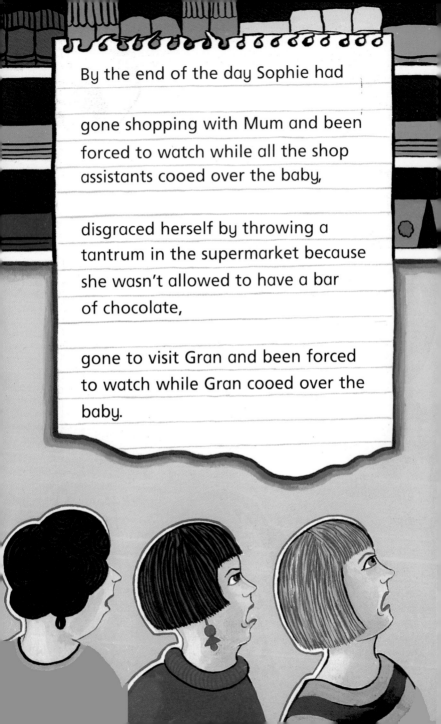

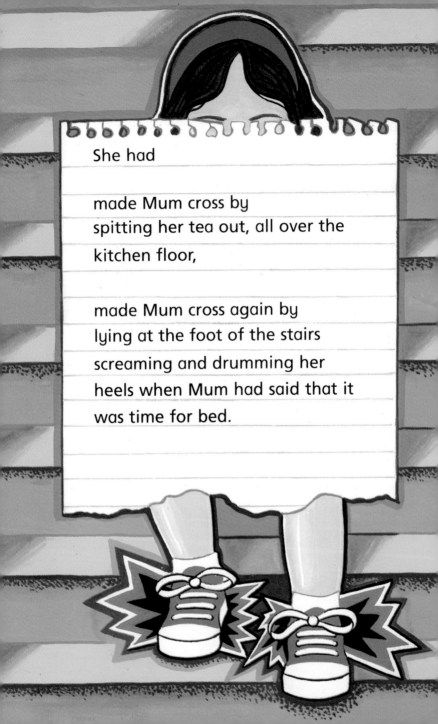

She had

made Mum cross by
spitting her tea out, all over the
kitchen floor,

made Mum cross again by
lying at the foot of the stairs
screaming and drumming her
heels when Mum had said that it
was time for bed.

("Don't want to go to bed!" yelled Sophie. "Dadda, Dadda! Don't want to go to bed!"

"Go to bed, Sophie," said Dad. "Do what Mummy tells you.")

"She's been like this all day," said Mum, and she dragged Sophie up the stairs, bump bump bump, holding her by the hand. Sophie roared and howled, but Mum took no notice.

"There!" she said, tucking Sophie away beneath the duvet. "You be a good girl and go to sleep and maybe tomorrow you'll wake up in a better mood."

"Shan't," said Sophie.

"Darling, do try," begged Mum. She bent down to give Sophie her goodnight kiss. "I love you just as much as I love the baby."

She didn't! It wasn't true! She never cooed over Sophie the way she cooed over that horrible smelly thing. All she ever did was smack Sophie for being naughty. It would serve Mum right if Sophie ran away!

## CHAPTER 2

In Sophie's bedroom, hanging on the wall where she could see it from her bed, was a picture of a lady in a floaty pink dress. She was standing by an empty cradle with one hand resting on the edge of the cradle and the other on her tummy, which was rather large and bulgy. She had what seemed to Sophie like a soppy smile on her face.

The picture was called Waiting for the New Arrival.

Mum had bought it for Sophie last year, when she had told her about the new baby that was going to come into the house.

"That's what we're doing," she had said to Sophie. "Waiting for the new arrival."

What she hadn't said was that the new arrival was going to be noisy and smelly and take Sophie's place. It wasn't fair! The baby got all the attention.

Sophie lay in bed, clutching her doll and her teddy bear and staring up at the picture. She wished that she could climb into the empty cradle and be the pink lady's baby. The pink lady had been waiting for her baby for months. She would be really glad to have Sophie. She would coo over her and cuddle her and tell her what a pretty little thing she was. And wouldn't Sophie's mum be sorry when she'd gone!

"That's what I'll do," thought Sophie, as her eyelids drooped. "I'll be the pink lady's baby."

## CHAPTER 3

Sophie was lying on her back, staring up at something round and shiny. What was it? Was it the sun? No, it was an electric light! What was the light doing on? Mum had switched it off when she left the room.

She turned her head on the pillow. Through the bars of her cradle – cradle? – she could see her bedroom, with its empty bed. How strange! Why wasn't she in it? She could see her doll and her teddy bear, but she herself wasn't there.

Now her mum was coming into the room and looking at the bed and calling "Sophie! Sophie! Where are you?"

And now her dad was coming in and they were searching all over the room – under the bed, in the wardrobe, behind the curtains – and Sophie wasn't there. Sophie was in the cradle, in the picture, hanging on the wall! And Mum and Dad were weeping and taking out their handkerchiefs and crying, "Oh, poor little Sophie! We have driven her away! Oh, why were we so mean?"

What a joke! Sophie tried to sit up and call out to them – "It's all right! I'm here!" – but to her horror she couldn't move. That is, she could wave her arms and kick her legs, but try as she might she couldn't sit up. And when she opened her mouth to call out – "Help! Help! I can't move!" – she found that she could only make silly gurgling  noises.

"Ah ah ah!" gurgled Sophie, thrashing in her cradle.

The lady in the pink dress came and bent over her.

"Kitchy kitchy koo," gurgled the lady, waggling her fingers at Sophie. Sophie stared at her, in outrage. What did she mean, "Kitchy kitchy koo?" That was baby talk!

"Gooo-ooo!" wailed Sophie, scrunching up her face.

"And goo goo goo to you!" said the lady, tickling Sophie under the chin. "Does oo want a cuddle, 'en?"

Next minute, to Sophie's indignation, she was being plucked out of her cradle and slung over the lady's shoulder.

It was such an insult. Here was Sophie, who could read, and write her own name, and count up to a hundred (almost), and here was the pink lady making fun of her. Using baby language. "Sha sha sha. Ma ma ma." As if she were about three months old. If this was what it was like being a baby, thought Sophie, then being a baby was horrible.

# CHAPTER 4

When Sophie woke up next morning it was a great relief to find that she could not only move her arms and legs but actually sit up and get out of bed. To prove how grown up she was she took off her pyjamas and put on her clothes all by herself, then went downstairs to find her mum.

"Hello!" said Mum. "What are you doing here?"

"I came to see if I can help," said Sophie.

By the end of the day, Sophie had

gone shopping and helped Mum
fill the shopping trolley,

looked after the baby while Mum
packed her shopping bags,

gone round to Gran's and helped
teach the baby to say "Nana",

gone back home and helped Mum
change the baby's nappy,

helped Mum give the baby a bath,

had a bath herself and put on her
pyjamas without waiting to be told,

talked (sensibly) to the baby while Mum made the tea.

("Hello, baby! How are you keeping? Are you well? You're looking very well, I must say.
And such lovely weather for the time of year!
Have you been away for your holidays yet?
Well, I must dash. I'm so pleased to have met you! Have a nice day!")

When Dad came in he said, "And how has Sophie been today?"

"Sophie's been as good as gold," said Mum. "I simply don't know how I should manage without her." Mum gave Sophie a big hug. Dad picked her up and swung her round. And nobody noticed the baby at all. Poor baby! Sophie ran over and waggled her fingers.

"Hello, baby! Say Nana for Sophie ..."